Clover's Secret

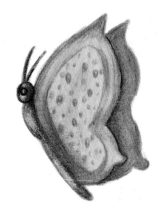

To Mom and Dad

Cover design and page layout by Circus Design

Library of Congress Cataloging-in-Publication Data

Winn, Christine M.
       Clover's secret / by Christine M. Winn, with David Walsh ; illustrated by Christine M. Winn.
              p.   cm.
       Summary: In an imaginary land where people can fly, two young girls form a friendship that helps one of them deal with the problems she faces at home.
       ISBN 0-925190-89-6 (acid-free)
       [1. Family violence—Fiction.   2. Friendship—Fiction.   3. Fantasy.]   I. Walsh, David.   II. Title.
PZ7.W72974C 1996
[E]—dc20   95-43559
                                                                                                  CIP
                                                                                                  AC

First Printing: March 1996
Printed in the United States of America

00 99 98 97 96   7 6 5 4 3 2 1

Published by Fairview Press, 2450 Riverside Avenue South, Minneapolis, MN 55454.

For a current catalog of Fairview Press titles, please call this Toll-Free number: 1-800-544-8207

Publisher's Note: Fairview Press publishes books and other materials related to the subjects of physical health, mental health, chemical dependency, and other family issues. Its publications, including *Clover's Secret,* do not necessarily reflect the philosophy of Fairview Hospital and Healthcare Services or their treatment programs.

The paper used in this publication meets the minimum requirements of American National Standard for Information Sciences—Permanence of Paper for Printed Library Materials, ANSI Z329.48-1984.

Clover's Secret

by

Christine M. Winn

with David Walsh, Ph.D.

illustrated by

Christine M. Winn

Fairview Press

Fairview Press

Minneapolis, Minnesota

In the village of Woobie, autumn was everyone's
favorite time. Every autumn, all the nine-year-olds learned
how to fly. And every autumn, Miss Jennie taught them.

This autumn, Miss Jennie gathered her new flying class around the Great Tree for their lesson.

"Okay, children," Miss Jennie called out on the first day. "Let's begin by giving everyone a flying buddy. Flying buddies watch out for each other in the sky." As Miss Jennie paired her students together, she noticed two girls who seemed like complete opposites. Clover was a quiet and shy little girl who stood far from the group. Micky, however, was right in the middle of everything, eager and alert. Miss Jennie decided that the two girls would make a good pair.

Every day the children followed their teacher's instructions. Some days they learned how to flap their wings. Other days they practiced gliding in the wind. And sometimes they worked on making a proper landing.

Everyone flew very well—everyone except Clover. She often became confused and made mistakes. When the group turned left, Clover turned right. She flew upward instead of gliding down. One time she missed the landing point and crashed into the village's mayor.

But Micky was a true flying buddy, and she was always right there to get Clover back on track. When Clover became embarrassed, Micky cheered her up. "It's okay, Clover," Micky said. "You'll be flying like an eagle in no time."

Micky was Clover's first friend.

"Hey, Clover, do you want to play pond tag?" asked Micky one day after flying lessons.

"Okay," agreed Clover. "But what's pond tag?"

"Follow me! I'll show you," said Micky. "You're going to love it!"

The girls spent nearly every afternoon at the pond, jumping and flying from lily pad to lily pad. Clover couldn't remember when she'd had so much fun.

"You're my best friend," said Micky.

"Micky, you're *my* best friend," said Clover.

One day, as the children gathered under the Great Tree, Miss Jennie said, "Class, it's time to explain something very important. How well you fly has more to do with your feelings than with your flying skills. On the days you feel good about yourself and your life, you'll be able to soar high above the clouds. But on the days you feel bad about yourself, you won't be able to fly your best." The children listened closely to their teacher as she spoke. "But remember, children," she said with a smile, "every day is a new start. Always look to the sky."

Micky thought a lot about Miss Jennie's message. "Something is wrong with Clover," she decided. "That's why she can't fly too well."

The next day, Micky started questioning Clover. "Is something wrong?" Micky asked. "You can tell me."

"No," answered Clover quickly.

"But I'm your friend," Micky continued. "I know something's bothering you."

"No," Clover said again. "I'm fine."

"But Clover, you aren't flying well," Micky persisted. "Maybe you should talk to your mom and dad. Maybe they can help you with your flying. I'll go with you to talk to them. I'd like to meet them. I've never been to your house and—"

"No, Micky!" Clover shouted angrily. "My parents don't fly. Just stay away from my house. Leave me alone, Micky. Just leave me alone." Clover ran off in tears.

Miss Jennie's last flying lesson prepares the children for a traditional Woobie ceremony. The teacher smiled with pride as she told the familiar story to her class. "In autumn, the Great Tree changes colors in a special way. Far up the trunk, the first layer of leaves turns purple. The next layer turns pink, then comes blue, and the very tip-top turns bright yellow. Each year, as the whole village watches, children fly as high as they can up the Great Tree and bring down a leaf."

The children tilted their heads way back to see the top of the tree, gazing hopefully at the bright yellow leaves. They loved the village tradition, but this year it meant much more—this year, it was their chance to fly.

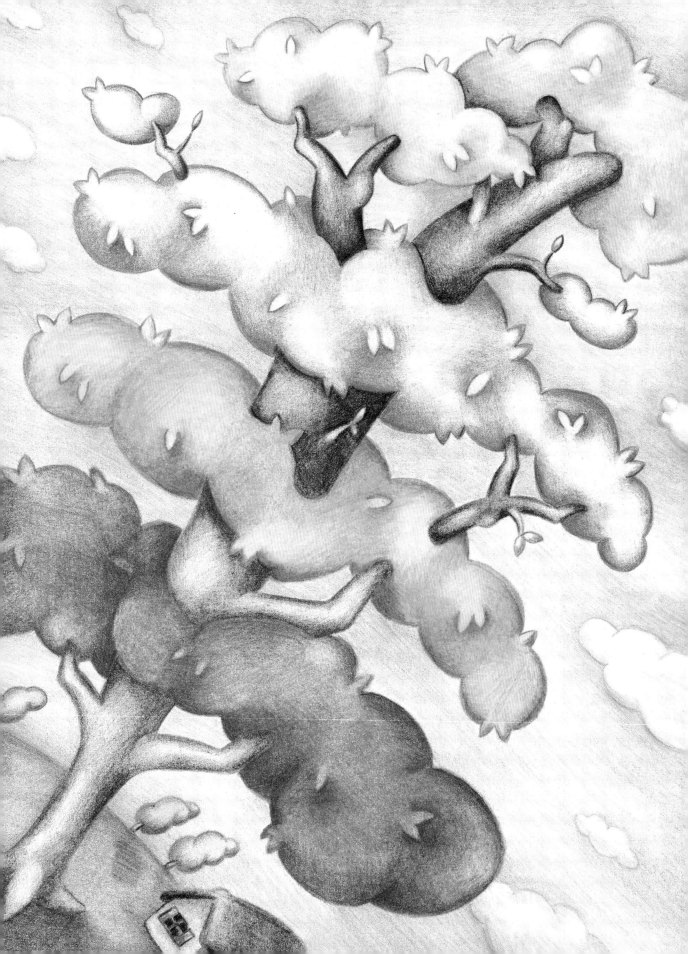

Everyone looked forward to the ceremony—everyone except Clover. As the ceremony got closer, Clover became even more quiet and her flying got much worse. Micky was worried about her.

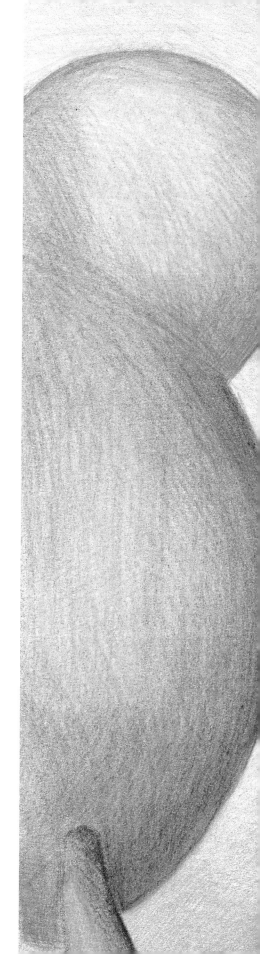

The flying ceremony was Woobie's biggest celebration. The center of the village was filled with music and dancing. Jugglers and clowns performed for happy crowds. Everywhere people turned were carts filled with treats to eat, like sugar Woobie cookies, maple syrup cakes, and breaded sausages on sticks.

Everyone in the village was there—everyone except Clover and her parents. Micky looked all through the crowd for her friend. When Micky flew up the tree and pulled her leaf, she looked for Clover from high above. But there was no sign of her.

When the celebration ended late that evening, Micky decided to look for Clover. "Something is very wrong," worried Micky. "No one ever misses the flying ceremony." She ran as fast as she could to Clover's house.

As Micky approached Clover's house, she could hear yelling coming from inside. Through the window shades she saw the shadows of her friend's parents. They screamed angry words at each other. And then Micky saw one of them begin to hit the other.

Micky froze in fright. She had never seen or heard anything so horrible. Just then she spotted her friend, curled up in a ball on the dark porch. Micky grabbed Clover's hand and the girls ran from the house together.

Micky made sure Clover was safe for the night. She carefully waited until the next morning before questioning Clover about what she saw.

"Clover, have your mom and dad aways fought like that?" asked Micky. "Has there always been hitting?"

"Yes," Clover whispered. "I didn't want you to see that. I didn't want anyone to know. Now you won't want to be my friend."

"Clover, we'll always be friends. No matter what, I promise," Micky answered. "But you have to talk to Miss Jennie. She'll help you. You can trust her."

"No, Micky," cried Clover. "I'm too afraid. I can't tell on my mom and dad."

"Please, Clover," begged Micky. "You need help."

Micky pleaded with her for a long time. Finally, Clover agreed to go to their teacher.

Miss Jennie listened to Clover tell about her parents fighting and hitting each other.

"You did the right thing by coming to me, Clover. I'll find help for you," promised Miss Jennie "There are people in the village trained especially to help families like yours."

"I'm glad I came to you, but...I'm still scared," Clover said.

"You're a strong little girl. You'll be fine in time," comforted Miss Jennie. "I'm always here for you, Clover."

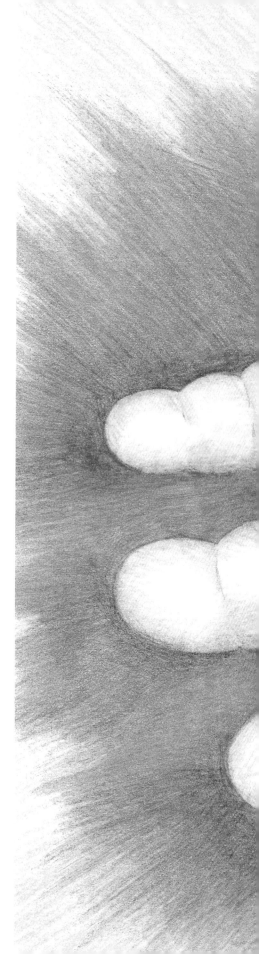

Micky found Clover later sitting by the pond. Micky sat down and put her arm around her friend.

"Are things okay now?" asked Micky.

"No, not yet, but maybe soon," answered Clover hopefully.

Then Clover opened her hand and showed Micky her purple leaf. "Next year I'm flying to the top," Clover smiled.

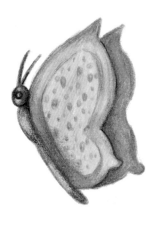

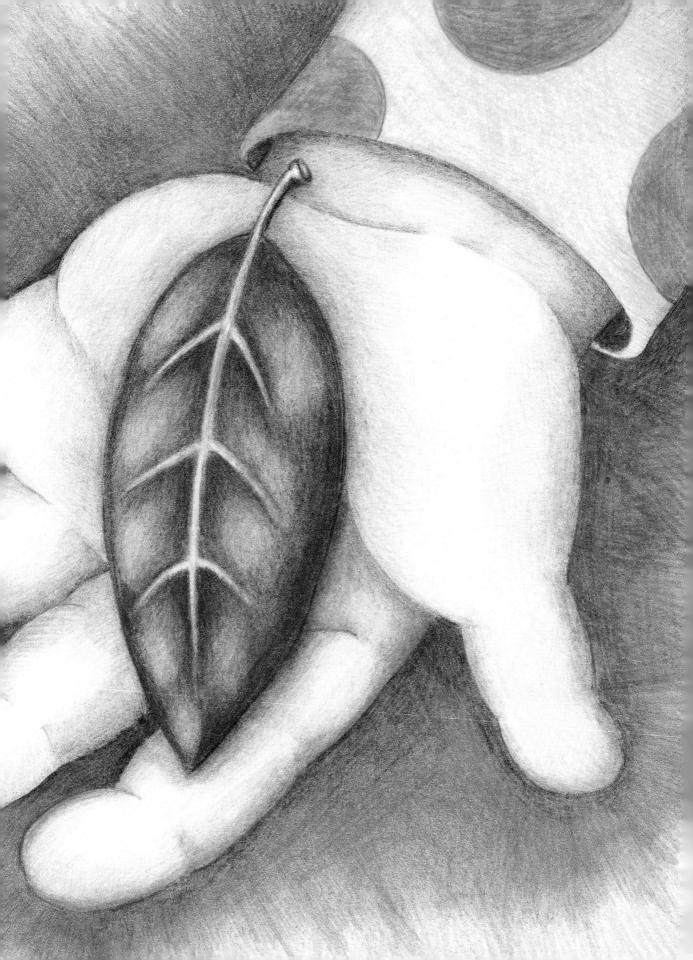

Other children's books by Fairview Press:

Alligator in the Basement, by Bob Keeshan, TV's Captain Kangaroo
illustrated by Kyle Corkum

Box-Head Boy, by Christine M. Winn with David Walsh, Ph.D.
illustrated by Christine M. Winn

Monster Boy, by Christine M. Winn with David Walsh, Ph.D.
illustrated by Christine M. Winn

My Dad Has HIV, by Earl Alexander, Sheila Rudin, Pam Sejkora
illustrated by Ronnie Walter Shipman